Shane's Mane

Nicole Drumheller Gargus

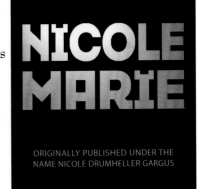

NICOLE MARIE

ORIGINALLY PUBLISHED UNDER THE
NAME NICOLE DRUMHELLER GARGUS

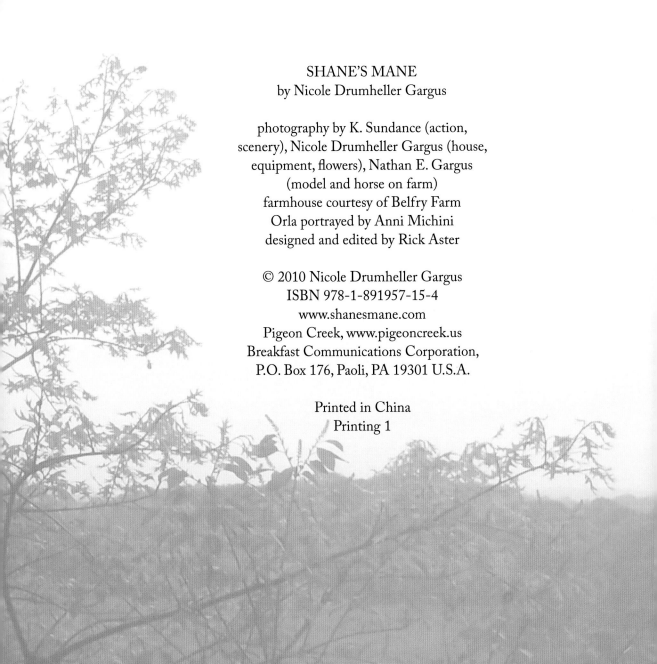

SHANE'S MANE
by Nicole Drumheller Gargus

photography by K. Sundance (action,
scenery), Nicole Drumheller Gargus (house,
equipment, flowers), Nathan E. Gargus
(model and horse on farm)
farmhouse courtesy of Belfry Farm
Orla portrayed by Anni Michini
designed and edited by Rick Aster

ISBN 978-1-891957-15-4
www.shanesmane.com
Pigeon Creek, www.pigeoncreek.us
Breakfast Communications Corporation,
P.O. Box 176, Paoli, PA 19301 U.S.A.

Printed in China
Printing 1

In memory of
Skips Holly Boy
Palomino Quarter Horse

4

T WAS SPRINGTIME. Outside, the birds were singing. The horses were out in their pastures. There were blossoms on the trees. But Orla was inside.

Orla was in the dining room. She was sitting with a book in her hands. The book was hard to read.

"I can't read, Grandpa," Orla said.

"You look like you're reading," Grandpa said.

"I can't read anything in this book," Orla sniffled. "How can you ever read something when you don't know what it says?"

"That's hard to explain," Grandpa said. "You read one word at a time, and then put the words together. What's that book you're reading?"

6

"I don't know," Orla said. "My teacher said I should read it for school. She said I'll never learn how to do anything unless I can learn to read a book by myself."

"Is that so?" Grandpa asked. "It seems to me you already do quite a few things. Haven't I seen you make a braid with your hair?"

"Grandpa! No one cares about that," Orla said. "I don't know how to do anything."

"Hmm," said Grandpa. He reached over to a shelf and pulled out another book. "Maybe you could read this book," he said. He handed the book to Orla.

Orla saw a horse on the cover of the book. She opened the book and looked inside. "This is a story about horses, isn't it?" she asked.

Grandpa reached down to turn a few pages. "Do you see how the word *horse* is all through this book?" he asked.

"Yes, I see it," Orla said. "But what are all those other words?"

"You will have to learn them," Grandpa said. "If you can learn the word *horse*, you can learn any word."

"But how?" Orla asked.

"Words are not so different from each other as they seem," Grandpa said. "They are all made from the same letters. They are all talking about the same world."

Orla had to think about this. Who had made so many words? How did they know what letters to use? Wiping tears from her eyes, Orla walked over to the window.

Orla opened the window. She smelled the fresh spring air. She could hear the sounds of horses. Orla looked out at Grandpa's green fields. She looked at the horses in the fields.

"Do horses know we call them horses?" she wondered. "Do they care about words at all?"

Out in the pastures, the horses were grazing, eating grass. Horses like to eat grass all day if they can.

One horse, though, was not eating. Shane had a pasture all to himself, but he did not seem to see the grass. Instead, he was pacing by the fence and shaking his gray mane.

Orla thought Shane must be sad to be kept all alone in his own pasture. Grandpa had told her that Shane did not get along with the other horses.

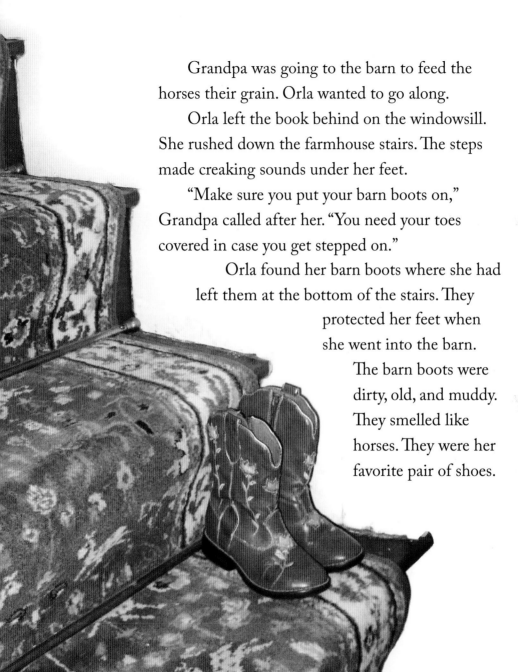

Grandpa was going to the barn to feed the horses their grain. Orla wanted to go along.

Orla left the book behind on the windowsill. She rushed down the farmhouse stairs. The steps made creaking sounds under her feet.

"Make sure you put your barn boots on," Grandpa called after her. "You need your toes covered in case you get stepped on."

Orla found her barn boots where she had left them at the bottom of the stairs. They protected her feet when she went into the barn.

The barn boots were dirty, old, and muddy. They smelled like horses. They were her favorite pair of shoes.

11

Orla followed Grandpa up the path to the barn. The old path was worn down by people and horses going to and from the pastures and the barn. Orla loved the way the ground felt under her boots.

Grandpa opened the gates. He whistled and the horses rushed to the barn. The horses went into their own stalls. Orla closed the doors behind them.

Grandpa opened the gate to Shane's pasture and chased Shane from the pasture to the barn. Orla ran after Shane and Grandpa. They all went into the barn.

13

14

Orla breathed in the sweet hay smell of the barn. The horses greeted Orla and Grandpa with nickers. A nicker is a soft sound a horse makes, like a whisper.

The horses watched Orla and waited. The grain was in a very large bag. The bag was too large for Orla to pick it up. Orla got grain from the bag in a scoop and poured it into the feeding pans. She put hay in the horses' stalls.

16

Then Shane began to whirl about in his stall and shake his head wildly again. He was neighing loudly. It was a sound that came from deep in his throat, like a scream. "He is worried he will be fed last," Grandpa said. "He is trying to tell us that he is the boss of the barn."

"Aren't you the boss of the barn, Grandpa?" Orla said.

"Try to tell that to Shane, though," Grandpa said. "He thinks this is his barn."

Orla stood on her toes and peered between the stall boards at Shane. Shane whirled again and again. He made a sharp neigh and kicked his stall door with a loud bang.

"Stay back from that horse," Grandpa warned. "He could hurt you!"

The days got
longer, and Grandpa
spent more time with
the horses. Orla loved
to watch Grandpa
ride, but she had
to stay out of the
way. She stood off
to the side with the
evergreen trees and
watched Grandpa
train his horses.

The trees around
Orla swayed lightly in
a warm spring breeze.
The breezes hinted at
the summer days that
would come when
spring was over.

Grandpa looked like a different person when he was riding a horse. It was not just the helmet on his head that made him look different. Sitting balanced in a saddle, his feet resting in stirrups on each side of the horse, his hands holding reins that connected to a bridle on the horse's head, everything Grandpa did was about the horse he was riding.

Today Grandpa was riding Shane at a full gallop! Shane was running as fast as he could go. Shane carried Grandpa on a trail through the fields. Mud and dirt went flying when they passed by.

One piece of muddy ground fell near Orla. Orla picked it up. In the mud, she could see the shape of Shane's hoof. Orla traced the shape with her fingers.

Watching from behind a fence, Orla tried to count the silver speckles on Shane's back. Orla wondered if Shane knew how much silver he had on his coat.

When the weather was warmer, Grandpa and Orla would send the horses out to pasture after they fed them at the end of the day.

Sometimes Orla sat under her favorite dogwood tree and looked at the horses and flowers. Just like horses, flowers came in different colors.

The blossoms on the dogwood tree were white. Shane too looked a little more white now that he had shed his winter coat. Yellow buttercups grew in the pastures. The horses ate the grass but did not eat the buttercups. Outside the fence there were purple irises.

Orla liked all the colors, but the purple flowers were her favorite. There were the tiny violets that grew in the grass, the irises with their long leaves, and the tall lilac bushes. Orla liked to walk under the lilac bushes on her way to the barn.

The sun was going down. It was time to go inside for dinner. Orla picked a few flowers to place on the kitchen table.

Even though Grandpa was a very good rider, he and Shane did not always get along. One day, Shane bucked up high and twisted hard to the right. Grandpa came out of the saddle and fell to the ground. Grandpa grumbled in pain. Orla thought he must be hurt.

"What happened, Grandpa?" Orla said, but Grandpa had already jumped up to his feet.

"I have to get right back in the saddle," Grandpa said. He adjusted the helmet that he wore on his head, and went after Shane.

Shane had stopped and was nibbling on some grass as if nothing had happened. Grandpa stepped back up into the saddle and went right back into a gallop.

Orla had been around horses for as long as she could remember.

Orla knew how to lead a horse around on a rope. She could pick up a horse's hooves one at a time to clean them. She knew how to brush a horse so its coat would shine.

Shane had his own red comb. Orla used the comb to smooth out the tangles of Shane's mane. Sometimes if Shane was going to a show, Orla would braid his mane the same way she would braid her own hair.

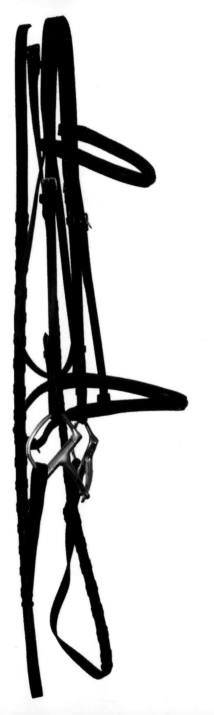

Orla loved the smell of Grandpa's saddles and bridles. Grandpa taught Orla how to put a bridle on a horse and showed her how it helped a person guide a horse.

He showed her how to put a bit into a horse's mouth and latch the bridle around the horse's nose and throat.

One day, Grandpa had Orla help him put his saddle on Oscar, a friendly dark chestnut horse. First they put a blanket on Oscar's back. They put the saddle on the blanket. Grandpa buckled straps under Oscar's belly to hold the saddle in place.

Then Grandpa put Orla in the saddle. Orla was up on a horse! She felt proud.

Grandpa led Oscar down to the end of the fence, then back to the barn. Oscar walked along with Grandpa, and Orla rode on Oscar's back.

Orla held on to the saddle. She wanted to go faster and ride the way Grandpa did — holding the reins and having the horse speed up and slow down and turn to the left and the right. But Grandpa was going slow.

Orla kept trying to read her books. But there were so many words, and Orla knew only a few of them.

One afternoon, Orla was in her bedroom looking at the book with the story about horses. On one page there was a picture of a girl walking across a creek, and Orla saw the word *feet*. "It is probably saying she got her feet wet," Orla thought. Orla looked at her own feet. It was a warm day, and she had no shoes on her feet. She was ready to walk across a creek too, she thought.

Orla looked at the page again. She tried to read what it said about the girl and her feet, but there were other words she did not know.

"I'll never be able to read this book," Orla said, "and then I'll never learn how to do anything!"

She put the book down on her chair.

Orla sat on the windowsill and looked out the window at the barn and pastures. Then she slid down from the windowsill and ran down the stairs and out the back door.

Orla walked alone
along the dusty path.
Dust from the ground
covered her feet
and slipped in
between her
toes.

Soon Orla found herself at Shane's pasture. Today, Shane looked calm and playful. He was trotting happily around the pasture. "Shane does not know how to read," Orla thought, "but it does not bother him."

Orla was sure she knew how to put a bridle on a horse. Maybe today she could put a bridle on Shane.

Orla walked on the tips of her toes into the barn. There were no horses around, but it still felt odd to be in the barn in her bare feet.

There was a box of apples. "I know Shane would like an apple," Orla said. Orla picked out the best apple and put it in her pocket.

Orla stepped up on a bale of hay to reach the black leather bridle Grandpa always put on Shane.

She lifted the bridle from the wall. Then she slipped it over her arm and shoulder and carried it back to the pastures.

Orla slipped through the fence and walked toward Shane. Shane stopped eating grass. He looked at Orla.

Soon, Shane's velvety nose was touching Orla's cheek. Shane lowered his head so Orla could touch his large floppy ears. Then Orla wrapped her little arms around Shane's thick neck.

Shane sniffed at Orla's pockets and nickered softly. He could smell the apple that Orla had brought him. Orla pulled the apple out of her pocket and gave it to Shane. Shane ate the apple, then rubbed Orla's shoulder with his head.

Orla slipped the bridle over Shane's head, then put the bit into his mouth. It was not as easy as it looked when Grandpa did it. Grandpa was at least as tall as Shane. Orla was not so tall. Shane had to hold his head down so Orla could reach it.

Orla thought the bridle looked right, and Shane seemed to agree. Orla fastened the buckles on the bridle. Orla looked at Shane. She saw that Shane was looking back at her.

Shane's bright speckled gray coat glowed in the warm spring sunshine. Shane's mane fell down around Orla.

Shane's mane was hiding her from the world, Orla thought. No one would be able to see her or see that she could not read, or that she did not know how to do anything.

"You are beautiful," Orla whispered. She looked into Shane's large dark eyes and felt the hot breath from his nostrils on her shoulders.

Orla pulled on Shane's mane to ask him to stay close. "I wish I knew how to ride a horse," Orla said.

Then Shane lay down on the ground next to Orla! Lying on the ground, Shane did not seem so big. Shane nuzzled Orla gently, and Orla climbed onto his back. Sitting on Shane's back, Orla could see how big Shane was. She ran her hands over the top of his large shoulders.

Shane stood up. Orla was still sitting on his back, but now she was up off the ground, the way she had been when she was riding Oscar. Shane looked back at her as if to ask, "Are you ready?"

Orla laughed. "Ready for what?" she said to Shane. "I don't even have a saddle!"

Shane started to walk around the pasture. Orla held on to the reins of Shane's bridle loosely. She looked down at her hands. Next to Shane's shoulders, her hands seemed very small. She looked down at the ground below. This far from the ground, she must be closer to the sky! Orla was happy at this thought, and she wished she and Shane could ride off to a magical place together — a place where children did not have to go to school and where horses were all that mattered.

Perhaps Shane knew what Orla was thinking, because he walked up to the pasture gate. Using his nose and teeth, Shane opened the latch. He gave the gate a firm push with his head. The gate opened. Just like that, they were out of the pasture! "How did you do that?" Orla asked Shane.

Shane was carrying Orla away. "Where are we going?" Orla asked. "I don't know how to ride. At least we should go to the barn to get a saddle if I am going to ride you. And I think I need a helmet, too." Orla never saw Grandpa ride without a helmet on his head. But Shane was going away from the barn.

"Shane, go back!" Orla said. She looked at the reins in her hands. Grandpa knew how to use the reins to tell a horse to turn around. But Orla did not know what to do, so she just held on to the reins. And Shane just kept going.

Shane knew the way through the woods and hills, along trails Orla had never seen. Soon the barn and pasture were nowhere in sight.

41

They came to a creek. Shane walked right into the water. Orla found herself in the middle of the creek, but she was above the water. Orla could not even reach the water with her toes.

Shane began to walk upstream, stepping slowly over the slippery rocks and pebbles. When he came to a deeper part of the creek, Orla held on tight. She felt the cold water flow around her toes, then around her ankles.

Shane reached out his right front leg and splashed in the water. Orla laughed. Shane then switched legs and began splashing with his left leg! Orla laughed and laughed as the water splashed around them.

42

43

"I don't want to get wet all over!" Orla said to Shane. It seemed that Shane understood this. He began to move on toward shallower water.

Sunlight sparkled
in the creek. Shane
went on upstream.
He left the water and
went back onto the
trail.

45

"I can ride a horse!" Orla thought. "I thought riding a horse would be hard, but this is so easy. Riding Shane is easier than the time I was on Oscar, and Shane is not going so slow. I wonder what other things that seem hard are this easy."

Orla had seen Grandpa press his heels to the sides of a horse to ask the horse to move forward or go faster. Orla's legs were not as long, but she tried to do the same thing. Shane began to trot — a steady, slow run for a horse. Then he began to canter — going at a faster running pace.

There were more and more trees along the trail, and then the trail went into a forest. The sounds of the forest were all around them. Orla heard the birds chirping and the leaves rustling in the trees.

The trees seemed to be whispering to them. Orla tried to hear the words they might be saying.

Shane went clip clop clip clop across a wooden bridge. Orla could hear the water babbling in the brook below.

They came to the edge of the forest. Orla could see the bright blue sky through the trees. Smaller trees grew along the edge of the forest, reaching toward the sun and the fields.

48

The trail went on along the edge of a long sunny hay field. Out in the open, Shane broke into a gallop and carried Orla racing across the green fields! Shane was barely touching the ground with his hooves.

The wind rushed around Orla's face and through her hair. Shane's mane flew freely in the air and swept across her face.

Orla did not care what she might do someday or how she would do it. She was riding a horse right now! She wanted to cry out, "Grandpa! I can ride! I can ride a horse!" but no one was there to see her. Instead, she just laughed.

Orla let go of the reins and stretched her arms up to the sky! She felt as if she could ride Shane all day. The wind rushed through Orla's long golden hair and Shane's silvery mane. Orla laughed again.

Meanwhile, Grandpa was not so happy. He saw that Orla was no longer in her bedroom. He could not find her anywhere in the house. She was not in the barn. When he looked in the pastures, the gate was open, and Shane was gone too. Grandpa became very worried. He looked everywhere for Orla and Shane. "Where could they be?" he grumbled.

Orla and Shane were on a path at the side of a field. Shane carried Orla right past lilac bushes. "I wonder if we are near the barn," Orla thought.

Shane trotted over the top of a hill, and Orla could see the barn. Then she saw Grandpa. Orla could see he was angry. Shane came to a perfect stop right in front of Grandpa.

"I told you to stay away from that horse!" Grandpa scolded. "He could hurt you! You do not even know how to ride!"

Shane looked at Grandpa and snorted like a dragon breathing fire.

Orla slid down from Shane's back before Grandpa
could lift her off. "I know how to ride Shane," she said.

Orla turned to walk into the barn. Shane followed
calmly with his head lowered between Orla's shoulders,
lightly touching her back.

Grandpa did not know what to say. He followed, shaking his head. Shane quietly walked into his stall.

"You at least should be wearing your barn boots and a helmet!" Grandpa said.

"I tried to tell Shane all of this, Grandpa," Orla said. "He took me for a ride! How can you get a horse to listen when you tell him something?"

"That's hard to explain," Grandpa said. "Horses have minds of their own. Did Shane do anything you told him to do?"

"Yes, a few things," Orla said, thinking. "But when I told him I didn't how to ride, he wouldn't listen. He just opened the gate and took off."

"That's one smart horse," Grandpa said, shaking his head again. "Did you tell him he is still not the boss of the barn?"

In his stall, Shane shook his mane, as if to say, "I got into the barn first, didn't I?"

Orla looked at Shane. "Shane, this is Grandpa's barn," she said. "You're just lucky he lets you come in here."

Shane just stood proudly and looked back at them.

"If you knew how to tell Shane a few things, then you could learn to tell him everything else," Grandpa said.

"Really?" asked Orla. "Can I? Can I learn to ride? I mean, for real?"

"You can learn to ride — but not right now," Grandpa said. "Right now, we have to feed the horses . . . and you're standing in the barn in your bare feet!"

Orla looked around. The barn did not look as big as before. It almost seemed crowded. Orla looked down at her bare feet, then looked around at the barn again. She thought of all the things that could happen to her feet in a place like this. She wished she had her boots on so she could feed the horses right now.

Orla looked at the bag of grain. On the bag, there was a picture of a horse, and then the word *horse*, and then . . . it must be the word *feed*!

"Grandpa!" Orla said. "The bag of grain — that says 'horse feed,' doesn't it?"

Grandpa looked at Orla. He looked at the big grain bag. He looked at Orla again. "Yes," he said, "that's what it says. It is called horse feed because it is what we feed the horses."

Orla was happy. She could ride a horse, and she would be learning more about how to ride. And she could read. At least, she had just read two words on a bag of grain. And if she could read a bag that was almost as big as she was, how hard could it be to read a little book?

Orla looked at Grandpa. "I will go get my barn boots right now," Orla said.

62

www.nicolewritings.com

Nicole Drumheller
Gargus grew up on
a small horse farm in
Pennsylvania. She writes
for magazines and
newspapers, often about
horses. *Shane's Mane* is her
first book for children.